# Turkey,

## *and*

# Twins

TWIN BLUEBONNET RANCH MYSTERIES

# Brittany E. Brinegar

# Contents

# About the Book

**They wanted a feast, but what they got was a mystery with all the trimmings.**
Twins Samantha and Lizzie hoped for a peaceful Thanksgiving in their charming Texas town. But when Lizzie's boss, a seasoned private investigator, entrusts her with a baffling case, their holiday takes a curious turn.

A priceless family heirloom, on loan to the museum, vanishes during the annual Pilgrim Pageant in front of hundreds of witnesses. Left in its place is Gobbles, the town Turkey, who every year gets a stay of execution for the holiday feast.

Lizzie suspects the elusive newcomer orchestrated the daring switcheroo. Tensions flared between him and her boss, when he attempted to purchase the heirloom the day prior. The case seems open and shut. But there's a hitch: the town newcomer has an unbreakable alibi.

Samantha and Lizzie are determined to leave no cranberry unturned as they unravel a web of secrets and prove even the tightest alibis can't hide the truth when the twins are on the case.

# 1 Hour Mysteries

Read More

# Chapter 1
# Long Black Train
## Samantha

A train whistle pierced through the nippy autumn air as we made our way across the crowded platform. My twin sister ducked between a pilgrim carrying a turkey and a man in an elaborate headdress, leaving me stuck in another time period. I caught an elbow in the side as I navigated around the ticket booth. Black smoke billowed from a chugging engine as the train slowed into the station.

I shoved through the crowd, concerned all these people may have lost their minds. Whatever happened to flying or driving in for the holiday? What was the sudden obsession with train travel?

Stepping over a pile of luggage, I jogged to catch up with Lizzie. She bounced on her tiptoes, scanning the faces of every traveler in search of our best friend. Instead of battling the masses, I leaned against the rock wall where I wouldn't be in the way. I tucked my hands in the pockets of my jean jacket as a bitter north wind threatened to knock me over. My cheeks and nose reddened from the chill.

Lizzie navigated the crowd with expert precision and flipped her homemade scarf over her shoulder. "I don't see her. Did you write down the arrival info correctly?"

"This is the only train until after Thanksgiving."

Lizzie blew into her furry pink gloves. "Maybe she missed her ride."

A woman pushing a baby stroller raced by me, running over the toes of my boots. I hobbled a few steps but didn't hold my breath for an apology. "Why can't people watch where they're going?"

"Do you think she's still on board?"

I lurched out of the way as a luggage cart barreled toward me. "Since when is Lake Falls Grand Central Station? Where did all these people come from?"

"Tourists?"

"Despite what the mayor says, our Pilgrim Pageant is not world renown." I shook my head as I spotted a film crew from channel seven. "Perhaps he's to blame for the spike in tourism."

Lizzie's gaze cut to her boss and mentor, Dr. Watkins. A woman applied powder to his nose as he prepared for the live interview. "You think all these people are here to witness the exhibit opening?"

"What exhibit?"

We twirled toward the voice of Becky Robinson. Lizzie wrapped her in a tight hug. "You made it."

I snatched her suitcase handle. "We better hustle. We parked in a loading zone."

"Samantha, that's no way to greet our dear friend who came all this way to spend her Thanksgiving holiday with us instead of partying with her Aggie classmates." Lizzie rolled her eyes. "Show some manners."

"Howdy, Becky. How was the train ride from College Station?"

Her hazel eyes sparkled. "Awesome… mostly? A little long." She bit her lower lip. "It wasn't quite as amazing as I thought. Television always makes it look more glamorous and romantic. Characters return home after a long time away, riding the rails and meeting interesting folk."

"That's a lot to expect, Beckers. It isn't a train from 1883," Lizzie said.

"I know. And it wasn't a total disaster. It's not like I returned home married to the wrong Walter Bishop."

Lizzie's brows knit together. "The who?"

I elbowed my sister. "It's a TV reference. We don't need to be bogged down by the specifics. Smile, nod, and move on."

"I'd like to know." Lizzie tilted her head to the side. "Who's the wrong Walter Bishop?"

"On *Moonlighting* Maddie Hayes returns home after months away and viewers think finally, we'll get back to the basics of what made the show fantastic. But instead of reuniting with David, played by Bruce Willis, it turns out she married a man named Walter Bishop – not the crazy scientist from *Fringe* – but a totally boring goof."

"Uh-huh."

I waved to Becky. "And this is why I skip pleasantries. That's two minutes of my life I'll never get back."

"I was going to make a joke about *Strangers on a Train* but figured that was too mainstream."

I held out my hand as Lizzie dropped a twenty-dollar bill in my palm. "Thank you."

"What was that about?" Becky asked.

"Side bet we made on the way over," Lizzie said. "She put money on the Hitchcock flick while I took *Back to the Future Part III*."

"Easy money."

Lizzie crossed her arms. "*Moonlighting* was million to one odds but no one took it."

"Anyway. Y'all were talking about an exhibit when I interrupted you." Becky squinted as the sun reflected off the sparkling red locomotive. "Is some famous painting on loan? Did thieves break in by cutting a circular hole in the glass ceiling and steal it?"

"Nothing quite so exciting as that but it's only Wednesday." Lizzie gestured to the news crew and Dr. Watkins.

"A few weeks ago, the doc bought a priceless journal at auction and he plans to reveal it during the Pilgrim Pageant tomorrow."

"What kind of journal?"

"It belonged to a passenger on the Mayflower," I said. "A teenager named Henry Samson."

"We're having a big reveal at the Wordsmith – red carpet, ornate glass display, the works. Business has been crazy all week." Lizzie frowned. "Which means I spent all of my valuable internship hours stocking shelves instead of cracking cases."

After retiring from Stanford's criminology department, Dr. Watkins bought the Wordsmith Bookstore and turned the upstairs apartment into a detective agency. Lizzie worked as his assistant in both aspects of the business, though her true passion was in the investigation side.

"And yet you expect me to believe the professor didn't grant you a sneak preview of the journal?" I asked.

Her eyes crossed. "Are you kidding? Dr. Watkins won't let anyone near the display. Especially me."

Becky pointed across the platform. "Who's the man he's arguing with?"

The news crew packed up their equipment and the doc traded in one interview for another. I focused on the stranger in the black cowboy hat. In a small town like Lake Falls, if you didn't know a person, they were at least familiar to you. "I've never seen him before."

"He's Ben McDuffie," Lizzie said. "The entertainer the town hired for the pageant. He sings and tells stories. A folksy guy. Everybody seems to love him."

"Everyone except Dr. Watkins." I cocked my head to the side. "I wonder what they're arguing about."

"Should I eavesdrop? You know, with my superpower?" Becky asked.

Lizzie waved. "Please do."

"I'm not as proficient at this as Doak but I'll give it a whirl." Becky zeroed in on their mouths and attempted to read their lips. "*No need to get upset friend. I am merely…* something…" Becky shook her head. "I didn't get the end. I think McDuffie wants to buy air or maybe loot?"

"An heirloom?" I asked.

She snapped her fingers. "Could be."

Dr. Watkins shoved McDuffie in the chest and pointed to the train tracks. Lizzie's eyes widened. "Doesn't take a lipreader to understand that message. The journal isn't for sale."

"Why would McDuffie want to purchase the pilgrim journal?" Becky asked.

"Dr. Watkins fielded at least a dozen offers since the *Gazette* ran the feature on his recently acquired treasure," Lizzie said. "It supposedly contains never before heard tales of the Mayflower. It is potentially a huge piece of history."

"If it's real."

All eyes shot to me and I shrugged. "The professor wouldn't be the first person to make a fuss for a publicity stunt."

"You said yourself, business is booming," Becky added.

"Y'all make it sound like he's P.T. Barnum." Lizzie flung her arms. "Dr. Watkins is far too proud to tarnish his reputation with a phony book."

"It was only a theory." I muscled Becky's heavy suitcase over the platform step. "Can we leave now? Assuming our car wasn't towed."

"The sheriff's department is taking the 'thirty-minute parking' designations way too literally," Lizzie said. "I spent thirty-one minutes at the market and got ticketed."

Becky grabbed my arm. "That reminds me, did Andi Montgomery win the emergency election?"

I stopped midstride. "You didn't hear?"

"No. Lake Falls gossip isn't a hot ticket item in College Station."

Lizzie cocked an eyebrow. "Well buckle up for a doozy because, against all odds, Andi and Durwood tied."

"How?" Becky's face flushed. "That can't be right. Deputy Durwood was way behind in all the polls."

"His stock rose after he helped us nab our bull nappers," Lizzie said.

I twisted my head to the side and studied Becky's guilty expression. "Please tell me you remembered to vote. You are still a resident of the county and therefore eligible."

"I voted." She cleared her throat. "But here's the thing…"

Lizzie's gaze lifted to the blue sky. "Uh-oh."

"Durwood is a bumbling deputy and everyone loves Andi. She's like a super cop. I didn't think the vote would be particularly close." Becky bit her lip. "In fact, I worried Durwood might be shut out."

"So, you voted for him out of pity?" Lizzie huffed. "We have to endure months of campaigning and debates because you felt bad for Durwood."

"The revote isn't until the spring," I said. "And in the meantime, Andi and Durwood are co-sheriffs. It's as messy as it sounds."

Becky covered her face. "What are the odds of an honest-to-goodness tie? I had no idea that was even possible."

"It's possible." Lizzie nodded. "The recount lasted weeks. I was tempted to sneak an extra vote into the box to be done with it until Samantha quoted the penalty for election tampering."

"I go away to college thinking nothing much will change." Becky sighed. "And then I come home to this – tied elections, Pilgrim journals, tourists. I've missed so much."

Lizzie threw an arm around Becky's petite shoulders. "The good news is you have a long weekend to make up for lost time. And with any luck, we'll stumble upon a mystery to solve."

# Chapter 2
# Pilgrim Pageant
## Lizzie

**Lizzie**

Thanksgiving Day arrived with a foreboding black rain cloud hovering over town and threatening to cancel the carefully planned festivities. I popped the collar of my tan peacoat as I navigated the Town Circle. Everywhere I looked volunteers scrambled to pitch tents and move decorations indoors.

Samantha grabbed my arm and tugged me forward. "We aren't volunteering for the decoration committee again."

"I didn't say we are."

"Yeah, but you got that helpful look in your eye."

"Only you can make pitching in sound like a character flaw."

Samantha's brown eyes narrowed. "We promised to finish all this town tradition stuff before the Cowboy's kickoff."

I tapped the dial on my watch. "Synchronizing now."

"How long do you think the grand reveal of the pilgrim journal will take?"

I gestured to the sky. "It depends on how much of a factor the weather delay is."

Samantha zipped her Ariat jacket and pulled the sherpa collar over her ears. "This scheduling conflict started in 1966 with the first Thanksgiving game and they've yet to work out the timing."

"Some might say the most important part of the holiday is not the Dallas Cowboys but spending time with family." Despite my best efforts, I couldn't hide my smile. "And those people would be wrong. I see no reason you can't care about both."

A droplet plopped from the sky and landed atop my head. I held out my hands, preparing for a sudden shower. But only one drop fell, further delaying the inevitable. We curved by the gazebo and thunder cracked in the distance.

"This is why you don't plan outdoor events in November," Co-Sheriff Andi said. "The weather is too unpredictable."

"I heard you the first twelve times, Andrea." Co-Sheriff Durwood scrunched his bushy mustache. "Stop playing Monday morning quarterback and lift your end of the feast table."

I checked my watch as we slipped into the movie theater. "We still have a little time to go backstage before the Pilgrim Pageant."

Samantha eyed the performer sitting center stage with a guitar. He told a joke as he strummed and the audience erupted in laughter. "McDuffie's not bad."

"Quite a bit better than the living art guy they hired last year. He was about as interesting as watching paint dry, which coincidentally is the name of his act."

McDuffie's fingers scraped across the frets as he changed to a g-chord. "Well, did y'all ever hear 'bout the time ol' Jed went out to wrangle ornery cattle? It was hotter than a branding iron in a blacksmith's forge that day, and we'd been ridin' for hours without a break.

"Now, Jed, he's got a knack for giving critters peculiar names. He spotted a stubborn steer and said, 'That there's Trouble.' Trouble sure lived up to his name, buckin' and twistin' like a tornado in a trailer park.

"Jed reckoned he could outsmart Trouble and pulled out a harmonica from his saddlebag. Well, Trouble must've fancied himself a music critic 'cause he stopped in his tracks, listening like he'd never heard a tune before.

"Jed played a sweet melody, and Trouble just stood there, hypnotized. We roped him easy as a snake in a boot, and Jed said, 'Now that's what I call a moo-sical interlude.'

"We had a laugh 'bout it, but I reckon Trouble thought he'd won in the end. See, he may have been a pesky steer, but he knew a good tune when he heard one."

He finished the story and broke into singing *Country Road Take Me Home*. Though people on the town council initially complained about McDuffie's folksy schtick, you couldn't deny he captivated an audience with a silly little story.

Samantha slipped behind the curtain and I hustled to follow her backstage. I dodged a costume rack barreling toward the dressing room, milliseconds before a pilgrim buckle stamped into my forehead. Other stagehands rushed back and forth carrying various props and set décor.

"Looks like there's a crisis," Samantha said.

I scanned the chaos. "Isn't this normal opening night jitters?"

"The Pilgrim Pageant is only a one-day show."

"And thank goodness for that. They haven't changed the script since 1995 and I'm pretty sure they stole most of the story from Disney's *Pocahontas*."

"A real person prior to the House of Mouse adapted the story," Samantha said. "They don't have dibs."

"Are you suggesting our *Shades of the Breeze* isn't familiar?"

"To what?"

"*Colors of the Wind.*" I rolled my eyes. "Forget I mentioned it."

"I would but I have an eidetic memory and never forget anything."

"You're a piece of work, Samantha." I smiled as I spotted Becky and her ex-boyfriend Boone Hitchcock in their pilgrim costumes. "Good morrow. How do ye fare?"

Boone removed his tall hat and bowed. "Jolly good, my dear."

I gasped and pointed to Becky's phone. "What be that device you hold? 'Tis like magic. Ye must be a witch. Where is me pitchfork?"

"I am no witch," Becky said. "This is arh… an egg timer for me pies. The buzz means they're ready."

I glanced at my stick-in-the-mud sister. "Aren't you going to get in on the fun?"

She frowned. "I wouldn't know where to begin. None of you are 'acting' in the same period. Lizzie jumped from the early 1600s to the Salem Witch Trials. Boone sounds like an inspector from Scotland Yard and Becky might be a pirate."

I stepped in front of her, cutting off further criticism. "So, when can we expect the curtain to lift?"

"The pageant is being pushed back until this evening." Boone adjusted his specs. "The mayor wants to finish all the outdoor festivities before the rain."

"He's about to pardon the turkey," Becky said. "We're heading over if y'all want to come."

"Of course. Sparing Gobbles is my favorite tradition."

We slipped out the back of the Royal Crown Theater and beat the crowd to the exit while McDuffie finished his set.

Boone stopped at a booth advertising miniature pump-kin pies. He fished out his money clip from his wool pilgrim pantaloons and removed a few bills. "Can I treat you ladies to a slice of pie?"

"Our family is cooking a feast at the ranch," Samantha said. "I don't want to spoil my dinner."

Becky's nose scrunched. "Do y'all have any flavors be-sides pumpkin?"

The kid behind the booth shrugged. "No?"

"I'll take one." I smiled. "Very sweet of you to treat, Boone."

He pushed his horn-rimmed glasses by the bridge. "Um, my pleasure, Lizzie."

I bit into the mini pie and nearly cracked a tooth. "Yum. Y'all don't know what you're missing."

A wry smile spread over Samantha's face. "That good?"

"Mmhh." I balled the rest of the treat in my napkin. "Heavenly."

Boone shoved his pie into his mouth in one bite and nearly choked. "Great pumpkin Charlie Brown." He spit out the pie into the bushes. "What is their secret ingredi-ent, rocks?"

"I'm more appalled by the pumpkin flavor," Becky said.

Before we reached the gazebo, the epicenter for offi-cial turkey pardoning, a brunette with long curly hair eased into our conversation. "Are one of you people Lizzie Brown by any chance?"

I waved. "Do you want an autograph?"

"Um, no…" The woman's brow furrowed. "I'm Christy Watkins."

"Oh, Dr. Watkins' sister." *What an awesome impression to make on my boss' relatives.*

"My brother is having trouble locating the red carpet and a cornucopia. He said you'd know where to look."

I nodded. "I do." I handed my purse to Samantha. "I'll be right back."

"Why are you giving me this?"

"Lizzie has all our snacks for the pardoning ceremony," Becky said as she grabbed the bag. "Don't be too long."

Christy clutched the lapels of her black blazer as we made our way across the windy Circle to the Wordsmith Bookstore. The fresh smell of rain hung in the air, putting a pep in her step. "Sorry to take you away from your friends on Thanksgiving."

"No biggie. I'm happy to help."

"When did you begin working for my brother?"

I arched a brow. "Over a year now. Wow, it seems like just yesterday I showed up at the store every day until he broke down and hired me as his intern."

"He said something about you joining the FBI."

"That's the dream after college. A recommendation from the doc would go a long way."

"You're lucky. He's an excellent teacher." A smile spread to her dark blue eyes. "Bill is quite a bit older than me and he already left the house by the time I started school but any time I had a problem with my homework, I'd call and ask him for help."

"He's proud of your accomplishments – big corporate lawyer in Boston."

"That's me." She tucked hair behind her ear. "So, I looked everywhere a cornucopia could possibly hide and nothing."

The door swung with a ring of the bell. The aroma of new and used books greeted me like an old friend.

"Christy, is that you?" Dr. Watkins peered over the balcony overlook. "Lizzie there you are. I've been looking all over creation for you. I can't find where you put anything and the town decided to move the schedule up three hours because of the blasted weather."

I opened the bench seat by the front window and retrieved the props. I didn't bother reminding the doctor
that I left him detailed instructions in his email. "I'll have
everything set up in a jiffy."

"You better. This is an important moment for the store."

Christy blew bangs from her face. "You're braver than
me," she whispered.

"He's all bluster… mostly."

After helping Dr. Watkins ready the store for the grand
reveal, I raced across the Circle in hopes of catching the
final few minutes of the turkey pardon.

A motorcycle lurched to a stop beside me and the
engine loudly idled. My eyes rolled as I recognized the
lime-green speedster. I made a last-ditch effort to try and
lose the driver but he already spotted me.

The helmet visor lifted to Dylan Fulbright's smug grin.
"Hey, pretty girl. Where you off to in such a hurry?"

I ignored his question and kept walking.

"What? You aren't even going to wish me Happy
Thanksgiving?"

Since moving to town to attend the university, Dylan
was nothing but a pain in the neck. He made passes at
Samantha and me mercilessly as if we were interchange-
able arm candy, despite the fact neither of us were remote-
ly interested in the frat boy.

"I guess my rugged good looks caused you to go
speechless, Brown." He smirked. "I do tend to have that
effect on ladies."

"Buzz off, Ivy League."

"You don't have to fight it. We both know you're madly in love with me."

I twisted on the heel of my furry boot. "What's my name?"

"Brown."

"My first name, Genius. Are you talking to Samantha or Lizzie? Do you even care we're different people?"

"Of course I know. You're the beautiful one." He winked and I felt like slugging him.

"Leave me alone."

Dylan parked his motorcycle and hurried after me. "I'm sorry, Lizzie. I have trouble appropriately expressing my feelings."

"Lucky guess."

"From the moment we met, I was enchanted. Nobody else in this sleepy hick town holds a candle to you."

"Then pack up your daddy's money and go back to where the pickings aren't so slim."

He ran a hand through his expensively styled blond hair. "I'm starting to wear you down. You like me a little bit."

"Get real, Ivy League. You may have weaseled your way into a few town events and committees but you're an obnoxious jerk."

"An obnoxious jerk with a pet name."

I stomped across the sidewalk and Dylan continued to follow. "Take a hint and leave me alone."

"I'm not following you, Miss Ego. I'm attending the turkey pardoning thing. If that so happens to be where you're going, it's a giant coincidence."

Irritation pulsed through my veins. My fist clenched and unclenched. *You can't give the rich boy a shiner on Thanksgiving.*

Boone stepped between us holding three caramel apples on sticks. "Is this guy bothering you, Lizzie?"

Dylan smirked. "And who's the little guy? Your boyfriend?"

I looped my arm through Boone's and kissed his cheek. "As a matter of fact, yes."

Dylan snagged one of the candied apples. "Is Samantha around here somewhere?"

I sighed when he stalked away, his stupid red leather jacket blowing in the wind. "Sorry about that, Hitchcock. I needed him to go away."

"That's okay." He cleared his throat. "Should we hold hands to keep up appearances or something?"

"Nah, Dylan's already bored with the chase. I think we're safe."

"Apple?" He shoved the sticky treat closer. "I promise it's better than that awful pie."

"I'm not much of a caramel fan."

"Me either."

"Then why did you buy three? Didn't want the other two to feel left out?"

"For juggling." The amateur magician tossed the two remaining caramel apples into the air and snatched them by the sticks. "It would be more impressive had that Dylan fellow not stolen one."

"He's the typical obnoxious trust fund frat boy bully who isn't used to people telling him no."

"Trust fund kids are the worst." Boone dusted lint from his bowling shirt. "Though there are a few exceptions."

I cringed realizing he caught a stray bullet from my insult. "Sometimes I forget you're rich, Hitchcock. And I mean that in the best way."

Becky waved from the crowd. "Y'all almost missed it. They're about to pardon the turkey."

I checked my watch. "They've been about to pardon the turkey for a half hour."

"Andi and Durwood forgot the paperwork. Each thought the other had it," Samantha said.

"At this rate, a write-in third candidate might win the job in a landslide." I crossed my arms. "Did the Governor call back in time or is Gobbles headed to the fryer?"

Becky's eyes widened. "Don't joke about that. He's an institution... she? Wait is Gobbles a boy turkey name or a girl turkey name?"

Folksy performer, Ben McDuffie, squeezed in beside me and tipped his cowboy hat. "Hope I didn't miss the big event."

"The way this is going, you probably had time for dessert," I said.

The audience clapped as the co-sheriffs and mayor finally concluded the ceremony with a bang of the gavel. The noise spooked Gobbles and his wings spread as wide as Shaq.

"He's on the move," Durwood yelled. "Get him."

"What are you pulling your gun for?" Andi asked. "We just finished pardoning him."

"Instinct." Durwood holstered his weapon and the crowd parted to allow the co-sheriffs to pursue Gobbles.

"Now that's what I call a turkey trot." McDuffie tapped out a rhythm with the heel of his boot and played the Bonanza theme on his harmonica. The spectators clapped along as we watched the chase from a safe distance. "Is every Thanksgiving this exciting?"

Samantha nodded. "Gobbles escapes every other year."

"Guess this means we have six more weeks of winter," I said.

McDuffie winked at me. "That's a good one. Mind if I steal it for my show later?"

"All yours."

"Do you think we should help?" Becky cringed as Durwood dove headfirst over the hood of a freshly waxed car.

Gobbles trotted away and Durwood hobbled, his trousers ripped at the knee. "They seem to be overmatched."

A bell rang across the street and Dr. Watkins addressed the crowd with a megaphone. "If you lovely folks will follow me, the Wordsmith Bookstore is proud to present a historical treasure."

I shrugged. "They got it. They're trained professionals."

Samantha's eyes darted to her watch. "We need to speed this along if we want to make it to the ranch before kickoff."

"I work most gamedays." McDuffie tapped his shirt pocket. "I never leave home without my little radio."

Dr. Watkins greeted everyone as we filed into the bookstore. His aristocratic Boston accent echoed through the rows of neatly stacked books. "Be sure to grab your complimentary apple cider on your way in."

Becky reached for a glass and I shook my head. She was far too clumsy to risk it. "If you spill a drop Watkins will ban you for life."

Her hand trembled as she set the cup back on the tray. "Good call."

Dr. Watkins beamed as everyone settled in and directed their attention to the glass display case covered with a red velvet sheet. "I am truly honored to share such a special moment with my friends and family on this marvelous holiday. It wasn't long ago…"

"Smoke," Christy Watkins screamed. "Fire!" She pointed to a thick dark cloud billowing from a building across the back alley.

# Chapter 3
# Gobble Meets Gumshoe
## Samantha

The outburst from Dr. Watkins' sister stunned the crowd. I twisted my neck and followed her point, not spotting smoke or fire. Thunder rumbled and a spark of lightning lit up the sky. An orange glow reflected in the window across the street.

"It's coming from the diner," I said.

Much to Dr. Watkins' chagrin, people charged outside. "Where are you all going? Don't you want to see the pilgrim journal?"

"If we don't extinguish the fire, it could take out the entire street," Lizzie said. "Including your shop."

"Where is your fire department located?" McDuffie asked.

I pivoted to the stranger. "Next to the school. Seven minutes away."

"Then we better get started." He removed his coat and addressed the crowd. "Folks, it was a dry summer and with all the leaves fluttering about, the street is a tinder box. Let's stop this thing before it gets worse."

Boone's nostrils flared. "Who put this guy in charge?"

"He's not wrong. This could get out of hand quickly." My boots clicked against the sidewalk as I raced to the nearby garden center for a hose. Being a reporter and an amateur sleuth made me skeptical by default but the timing of the fire was nothing short of suspicious.

Lizzie followed and untangled a knot in the hose. "The fire is on the roof. Isn't that a little odd?"

"Not unusual for a lightning storm." I wrapped the hose around my arm. "These things happen."

"I guess." She grabbed the other end and helped me haul it to the front lines. Her eyes darted as she watched the crowd, waiting for the other shoe to drop. "I think this might be arson."

"Who would have a beef with Nifty Fifties?"

"Maybe someone ruined their turkey and is mad the diner is closed."

"Or this is a distraction for something bigger." I bit my bottom lip and scanned the chaos.

McDuffie and some of the other guys took the lead and controlled the flames until the fire department arrived. Sirens echoed in the distance, letting everyone know help was on the way. But as we passed buckets of water back and forth, I couldn't shake the thought that someone started the fire.

The local shops were closed but they were all stocked with Black Friday merchandise. Could they be targets of a thief? I shook away the thought. Jumping to conclusions was detrimental for an investigator. I needed to examine the evidence before forming theories.

I glanced over my shoulder at the bookshop. Dr. Watkins stood in the doorway barking orders. He clutched a fire extinguisher in case the flames jumped the street.

Lizzie grabbed me by the arm. "I just talked to Durwood. Initial assessment is the fire originated on the roof."

"Lightning?"

"Off the record, he didn't think so."

The crowd cheered as the firefighters extinguished the last of the flames. "We got lucky folks," Andi said. "The fire burned hot and bright but it was easily contained."

"Thank you to everyone who acted swiftly." Durwood shook hands with McDuffie. "Give a hand to the Thanksgiving hero!"

McDuffie wiped soot from his forehead. "I didn't do anythin' special, Sheriff. It was a team effort."

"And modesty to boot." Durwood slapped the man's back. "How about we go get some chow? I hear there's a feast waiting in Town Hall."

Dr. Watkins marched into the heart of the action, waving his megaphone. "Durwood, you buffoon, we haven't finished here."

"Is there another fire?"

"I'm trying to bring a bit of culture to the town with the pilgrim journal." He gestured to the red carpet. "We were in the middle of the grand reveal when everyone ran outside."

Durwood rubbed his belly. "I guess the food will stay warm."

"This is something everyone has been looking forward to for weeks," Watkins said. "It's not as if I'm twisting any arms."

We filed back inside with a thicker crowd than the first attempt. Dr. Watkins started his speech from the top and I tuned him out.

Becky tiptoed and craned her neck to look at my watch. "At this rate, I don't think you're going to make kickoff."

"Any chance we can bail?"

Lizzie shushed me. "He's removing the cloth."

As a writer, I loved books and history but the ceremony and multiple delays made me indifferent. Besides, how much could we glean from a journal encased in glass? It wasn't as if we could thumb through the pages and read about Henry Samson's journey.

The spectators gasped and I wondered what I missed daydreaming. Christy Watkins removed the velvet sheet but instead of revealing a journal from the seventeenth century, she was nose to beak with Gobbles.

"What's a turkey doing in there?" Watkins yelled.

Lizzie lowered her voice. "Where's Hitchcock the Magnificent? This has his sticky magician fingers all over it."

He leaned around a bookcase. "It wasn't me. I swear."

"Are you sure?" Becky asked. "Because replacing a priceless artifact with a turkey sounds like one of your magic tricks."

"I was with y'all the whole time," Boone claimed.

As the doctor called for the sheriffs, theories ran through my mind. "It might not have been Boone's trick but someone is behind this misdirection. The fire was the distraction."

Lizzie nodded. "While everyone looked the other way, someone made the switcheroo."

"Who?" Becky's eyes darted. "The journal is super valuable, right? It could be anyone."

"What do you mean you're taking me in for questioning?" Dr. Watkins jerked his arm away from Co-Sheriff Andi. "I'm the victim here."

"Maybe, maybe not." Durwood leaned closer. "That's what we intend to find out."

"You morons. Someone could be fleeing the city with my property and you're both escorting the old man across the street to the station?" He flashed a thumbs up. "Brilliant police work."

Lizzie crossed her arms. "I better go with him before he says something he regrets."

"We'll search for clues and talk to witnesses," I said. "Let us know if you learn anything."

# Chapter 4
# Stuffed or Cuffed?
## Lizzie

I trailed Dr. Watkins to the station, catching a few strays as he yelled at the co-sheriffs. "None of this would have happened if you readied the store yesterday like I asked, Miss Brown."

A muscle in my jaw tensed. I didn't like being called out, especially when I did nothing wrong. I probably should have taken my lumps and stayed quiet, but it wasn't in my nature to avoid conflict. "How are you blaming me right now? I've never even seen the journal."

"Never seen the journal?" Durwood's bushy eyebrows rose. "Fascinating. Does this pilgrim diary even exist?"

Dr. Watkins stroked his white mustache. "You've done quite enough, Miss Brown. I won't require further assistance."

"Good call, Bud. The nosy teens just tend to get in the way." Durwood blocked my path into the interrogation room. "You don't go beyond this point without a badge."

I pulled Andi aside before she followed them. She was always more reasonable and helpful than her counterpart. "Is it just me or are y'all treating Dr. Watkins as a suspect?"

She swatted long, curly black hair over her shoulder. "Paul, the insurance guy, let it slip that the doc upped his policy yesterday. Then the priceless journal no one has seen goes missing the next day... let's just say we have questions for your boss."

"Can I sit in?"

"Not today, Lizzie."

My lip curled. "I expect that from Durwood but I thought we were friends, Sheriff."

Her lanky body slumped. "Ugh, fine. You can watch from observation with my uncle. He can use the training." She winked at the young, rookie deputy. "Keep her in line, Doak."

He placed his felt Resistol cowboy hat upside down on the desk. "Yes ma'am."

In one of those unusual family dynamics created by a second marriage, Andi was almost a decade older than her uncle, Doak Walker Montgomery. He joined the sheriff's department while taking night classes in criminal justice at the junior college.

"Does this have something to do with the fire?" Doak asked.

I shook my head. "Dr. Watkin's journal is missing."

He released a low whistle. "Yikes. Well, if you need a job, we always have openings."

"Funny but it wasn't my fault. Watkins didn't let anyone else touch the journal."

"We both know he'll find a way to blame you." He opened the door to the observation room. "Why are they treating him like a perp?"

"Something to do with the insurance policy." I plopped into the uncomfortable chair and stared at the room on the other side of the glass.

Doak clicked on the sound. "What do you think?"

I shrugged. "Committing insurance fraud one day after upping the policy is sloppy."

His head bobbed as he picked up on my thread. "And if there's one thing the doc isn't, it's sloppy."

On the other side of the two-way mirror, Durwood coughed on his coffee. "You insured a dusty old diary for a million bucks? I have a lightsaber from the *Return of the Jedi* that isn't worth half that."

Watkins removed his glasses and cleaned the lenses. "If there was a question in that blubber, I missed it."

"Care to explain why the item is over-insured?" Andi asked.

"I don't happen to think it is." He pounded his fingers into the metal table, his Boston accent intensifying with each syllable. "This is a piece of American history we are talking about. You can't put a price tag on that."

"Apparently you can for a million bucks." Durwood slurped his coffee. "You could make it disappear, sell it on the black market, and keep the insurance dough. The perfect crime."

"If you think that's a perfect crime, you have less business being co-sheriff than I thought." Watkins crossed his arms over his wool sweater. "You two geniuses are wasting time with me when the thief is getting away with my property."

Durwood held up a hand. "Cool your jets, Gramps, and let us ask the questions."

"Gramps? Resorting to name-calling, are we?"

"You started it with the genius insult."

"For accuracy's sake, would you prefer dummy, dunce, nitwit?"

Andi cleared her throat. "Dr. Watkins, what prompted you to up your policy?"

"You people forget, I'm not just some book guy. I've been doing this type of work, interviews, longer than you've been alive."

"As a professor." Durwood snorted. "And now your assistant does all the crime solving."

"I run a successful detective agency and I'm a respected member of the law enforcement community. I didn't steal my own property."

"Who did?" Andi asked.

"I'd like to find out." Dr. Watkin's pinched the bridge of his nose. "I upgraded my policy on my sister's insistence. She didn't think I should put the journal on display in my store where anyone could walk in and nab it. But knowing I'm stubborn and would ignore the risk, she urged me to properly insure it. But what the gossip Paul might not have explained to you is the policy won't go into effect until tomorrow, after the holiday. I'd be a dumb thief to snatch it a day early."

"Interesting." Durwood knocked on the table. "Hang tight while we check your story."

"I'll be waiting."

"What do you think, Lizzie?" Doak twirled his cowboy hat and bounced his knee. "Still think your boss is innocent?"

"You don't?"

"Why has no one else seen the journal?"

"Because he wanted to drum up business with a grand reveal."

He ran the pad of his thumb over his eyebrow. "And what about the sister?"

"I'm more interested in McDuffie."

Doak stretched to his full height of six-foot-four. "The traveling performer? Why?"

"We overheard a fight between him and Dr. Watkins yesterday. McDuffie offered to buy the journal."

"And?"

"That's suspicious."

"Why exactly is that suspicious?"

"Maybe McDuffie didn't take no for an answer."

Doak spread his arms. "Then let's talk to McDuffie."

"Teeney problem." My lips curled. "He has an alibi for the crime."

"An alibi isn't insignificant, Lizzie. Who can verify it?"

"Me, Samantha, about fifty other people who watched him play hero and put out a fire."

"That is a problem."

"Unless he has an accomplice."

"The guy has an irrefutable alibi, a flimsy motive, and everybody likes him." Doak tossed his shoulders. "Let me draw up the arrest warrant now."

"No reason to mock. My gut tells me the guy is up to something."

Doak flashed a wry smile. "Is it the mesmerizing stories or the angelic voice that tipped you off?"

"Who hired him?"

"Town council."

"How did they hear about him?"

"I think he answered our ad in the paper for a performer."

I snapped my fingers. "See? That's odd."

"Not really."

"He wasn't recommended. He's a stranger who showed up."

Doak's brown eyes narrowed. "And he just so happened to know about this priceless pilgrim journal?"

"We advertised the Wordsmith's grand reveal in the newspaper."

"A coincidence."

"One that might turn into a connection."

He rubbed the stubble on his chin. "Alright. I'm willing to take a leap with you."

"Excellent. But just in case I'm wrong, I'll call Samantha and put her on the sister angle."

# Chapter 5
# Count Your Blessings
## Samantha

**Samantha**

While deputies ushered people outside the Wordsmith, I took a closer look at the glass display case where the journal transformed into a turkey. "How did they make the switch?"

Boone stroked Gobbles' feathers, a laughable sight considering his pilgrim costume. "The lock wasn't tampered with."

"Are you sure?"

"I'm a magician. I can tell when a lock has been picked."

"Whoever made the switcheroo did it between the turkey pardoning and now," Becky said. "Not a huge window."

I hunched over and shined my flashlight on the display case. "Someone wiped the glass clean of fingerprints."

"What about the cop who let Gobbles out?" Becky asked.

"He wore crime scene gloves." I inspected the lock closer. "If it wasn't picked, then the thief probably had a key."

"I hate to bring this up since Lizzie looks up to the doc, but is it possible the journal is a hoax?" Boone asked. "Did anyone ever see it?"

"I did additional research last night. It's real."

Lines formed on Becky's forehead. "What sort of research?"

"I took a peek at the ticket from the auction house. Dr. Watkins spent a lot of money to procure the journal."

"Is 'took a peek' code for hacked into the auction house?" Boone asked.

"No."

"I think it is." Boone shifted, attempting to stand a little taller. "We're all friends here, Samantha. You can tell us the truth."

"Most of the information was public record." I lifted my shoulder. "And the rest wasn't very secure."

"Alright, so we can assume the journal exists and that someone really did take it." Becky narrowed her gaze. "Now what?"

Boone grabbed a magnifying glass from the bookshelf. "We search for clues."

"In an old-timey cartoon? Ditch the magnifying glass."

Boone raised his eyeglasses and peered through the cliché detective prop. "Ye of little faith. I already found something."

"What?" Becky asked.

He plucked something from the carpet. "Little crumbs embedded in the fibers." Gobbles pecked at his hand. "Ouch, he likes it."

"Turkey feed." I leaned on the bookshelf. "Probably how the culprit lured Gobbles into the glass case."

Boone scooped up the bird. "I wonder if the feed store can give us a list of customers who purchased turkey feed in the last few days. Then we can cross reference that with people who were nearby before the fire."

I rotated my neck as I wondered how I got stuck on the team with the magician. Occasionally he was helpful but in a time crunch, his antics slowed me down. A scheme came to me and I put on my best poker face. "That sounds like a theory Lizzie would come up with. She loves hitting the pavement to look for leads."

"She and I think alike."

"Why don't you investigate that?"

He beamed. "I'm happy to."

"And take Gobbles as part of your cover story."

He flashed a thumbs up. "Brilliant."

Becky crossed her arms and a smug smile spread from ear to ear. "I guess I'm not the only one who knows about Boone's crush."

"Doesn't everyone?"

"Lizzie doesn't."

"You're kidding? But it's so obvious."

"To everyone but her."

"Huh. For a detective, she's sometimes quite clueless."

Becky frowned. "So why did we ditch Boone?"

"We didn't ditch him."

Her face twisted. "I'm certain you don't see any merit in his turkey feed theory."

"Of course not. This time of year, he'd have more luck finding someone who didn't purchase turkey feed." I spun on my heel, wanting to clarify. "That's hyperbole to make a point the list will be substantial and likely unhelpful."

"I caught that subtlety."

I tapped my lip with my forefinger as I paced. "Was anyone missing from the fire?"

"I don't know." Becky lowered her voice. "But remember yesterday at the station? We overheard Watkins and McDuffie arguing about buying the journal."

"I remember, I never forget anything. What about it?"

"It makes the troubadour look quite guilty."

I shook my head. "He didn't have time to make the switch. He was front and center, fighting the fire."

"What about Christy?" Becky asked. "I don't remember seeing her during the chaos."

A text message glowed across my phone screen. "Lizzie just presented a similar theory." I handed her my phone so she could read it for herself.

"Always suspicious when someone raises an insurance policy." Becky bounced on her toes. "Wonder where we can find Christy."

The bell rang and a deputy glared at us. "Everyone is required to clear out until the sheriffs return to process the scene."

"Really?" Becky asked. "But the sheriff told us to hang back and help."

"We're supposed to take Christy Watkins on a walk-through of the crime scene, make sure nothing else is missing."

The deputy's eyes narrowed and he dipped his chin. "You're sure you cleared this with the sheriffs?"

Becky spread her arms. "How many times have we helped the sheriff's department crack cases? Our help in the bull napping almost got Durwood elected."

"We're practically on the payroll."

He scratched his head and disappeared outside. A few seconds later, he returned without Christy. "She's gone."

"What do you mean gone?" I asked.

"She left."

Becky lurched away from the counter. "Weren't y'all keeping an eye on her?"

"What for?"

"To interview witnesses," I said.

The deputy tossed gloved hands. "They all said the same thing. Turkey appeared out of nowhere. Didn't figure I needed to write up thirty different statements repeating one collective story."

I rubbed my eyes. "Christy is visiting from Boston so she's either staying with her brother or at a hotel."

Becky nodded. "You think she went home?"

"We know she didn't go to the police station. Lizzie would have seen her."

Becky raced around the counter and disappeared behind the register. She popped back up with a thick phonebook. She dropped the book with a thud and the lamp and computer trembled like they were hit by a mini earthquake. "I'll find Dr. Watkins' home address while you call the Country Corner Inn and see if Christy is a guest there."

"She's a guest."

"How do you know? You didn't even call anyone or hack anything."

I pointed to a disposable coffee cup with the inn's insignia. "Those are only given out with the complimentary breakfast."

"Okie dokie then." Becky gave me a double thumbs up. "Gold star for the hyper-observant."

Becky and I jogged the four blocks to the Country Corner Inn and arrived just in time to catch Christy shoving bags into the only taxi in the county.

Becky twirled her colorful umbrella. "She's fleeing town!"

I grabbed her last duffle bag before she could stuff it in the trunk.

"What do you think you're doing?" she asked.

The elderly driver leaned out the window and scratched his prominent bald spot. "Is something going on here?"

"Step on it quick," Christy said as she opened the cab door.

Becky stepped in front of the car and posed like a superhero. "Cut the engine, Edward. She's not going anywhere."

The driver didn't listen and edged forward. Becky slipped on a puddle and almost twisted her ankle on the curb.

"Sorry, but this is my first fare in over a year. I don't want to blow it."

"Fine. Just know the sheriff will come after you as an accomplice for driving the getaway car."

The brakes squealed and he stopped the meter. "That will be ten cents."

Christy barreled out of the car and slammed the door. "You people are a bunch of kooks."

"Why are you fleeing town?" Becky asked.

"I'm not fleeing." Christy tightened the cinch on her trench coat. "I'm just leaving."

"Twenty minutes after a priceless journal disappears and your brother is arrested?" I raised an eyebrow. "Your timing is impeccable."

"Bill was arrested? On what grounds."

"Insurance fraud," Becky said.

Christy plopped on the front stoop. "This is just perfect."

My eyes scanned her various bags. One of them might be concealing the pilgrim journal. "Why are you leaving town in such a hurry?"

She blew a curl out of her face. "Because I'm a jinx."

"I beg your pardon?"

"Why are you a jinx?" Becky asked.

"The only thing I'm good at is making a mess of my life and everyone else's." Christy blubbered into a tissue. "This isn't the first time, either. I'm not even a lawyer. I'm a legal secretary who can't make a decent score on the LSATs but I never even told my brother. I created a phony backstory about law school and photoshopped graduation pictures. I'm a fraud."

She was fragile and on the verge of confessing. I needed to proceed with caution. "What happened today?"

"My brother wanted to display the pilgrim journal and I told him it was a bad idea but have you ever tried to convince someone as stubborn as him to do something?"

Becky's gaze darted to me. "I have some experience, yes."

"His mind was made up." Christy's voice cracked. "So, I insisted on watching the journal from the moment we put it in the case until we locked it in the safe again. I wasn't going to take my eyes off it. Not for sweet potatoes, cranberries, or a slice of that wonderful pumpkin pie your town is famous for. And then that stupid fire happened. I lowered my guard and some thief slipped Gobbles in the display case. As if to rub my nose in my mistake. The only explanation is I'm a jinx."

I blinked, unsure what to make of her admission. Unless the breakdown was an act, she didn't appear put together enough for a heist. "We can help you make up for your mistake."

"How?" She blew her nose like a congested elephant.

"We're detectives," Becky said. "Sorta."

Christy glared at us, skepticism radiating from her intense eyes. "My brother wasn't wrong when he called you all Nancy Drew, was he?"

"If that's supposed to be an insult it's a terrible one," Becky said. "We're Nancy's biggest fans."

Christy tugged on her coat. "Listen I don't care if you guys are twelve. If you think you can somehow find the journal and help me make amends, I'll answer whatever ridiculous questions you throw my way."

"Can you think of anyone who might want to steal the pilgrim journal?" I asked. "Someone who might benefit from taking it."

She jerked backward. "It's a valuable item. Who wouldn't benefit?"

"Does anybody specific come to mind?" Becky placed a hand on her shoulder. "Did you notice someone lurking around the bookstore in the last few days?"

Christy shoved frizzy hair from her face. "That singing storyteller was overly interested in the journal."

"McDuffie?"

She nodded. "He wouldn't take no for an answer and kept pushing. But at least two zeros were missing from his offer. He started to bug my brother."

"Thank you for your time," I said.

"And don't leave town," Becky added. She tugged my sleeve as we headed down the sidewalk. "McDuffie tried to buy the journal. That's the same thing they argued about at the train station."

"I know." I chewed my lip. "Guess we better see if Lizzie had any luck with our top suspect."

# Chapter 6
# Feather in Your Cap
## Lizzie

**Lizzie**

After leaving the police station, Doak and I spent the better part of twenty minutes searching for McDuffie but no one had seen him since the fire. My stomach knotted as my suspicion intensified. If I was right about the troubadour, he might be halfway to Mexico with the pilgrim journal.

Raindrops pelted the brim of Doak's cowboy hat like a gunslinger in a western. "He's due back on stage in fifteen minutes. He likely didn't go far."

"Unless he isn't sticking around for the matinee."

"The rain's getting worse. Maybe we should go inside the theater and wait for him to show."

I squinted at the sky as droplets drummed against my umbrella. The thick gray clouds showed no signs of letting up. My brow furrowed as I spotted movement on a roof. A dark shadow in a cowboy hat leaned over the edge, watching the town below. I followed his sightline to the gazebo, unsure what he found so interesting.

My boots splashed in a puddle as I raced across the street to the pharmacy. "Someone's up there."

Doak tilted his hat. "Is that McDuffie?"

"Sure looks like him."

"What's he doing up there?"

"Starting another fire?" I ran around the two-story brick building. "How do we access the roof?"

Doak snagged my umbrella hook and stretched for the fire escape ladder. When I tried to climb on first, he held up a hand. "Let's pretend for a second I'm the cop in this scenario."

"You're a rookie deputy in training."

"And I outrank a college student who interns for a private eye." He spit in his palms for a better grip and hustled up the ladder. "When you finish Quantico, I promise to let you go first."

The iron ladder mixed with rain to produce an overwhelming rusty, metallic odor. "What do you suppose McDuffie is doing on the roof?" My hand slipped and my boot missed a railing. I clutched the slick bar with all my might.

Doak showed off his balance by leaning backward and holding on one handed. "Are you okay down there?"

"Peachy." I sucked in a breath and continued to climb.

He reached over the edge of the roof and pulled me up. "Why don't we talk to him instead of theorizing endlessly?"

I brushed a hand over my peacoat as I carefully traversed the roof. McDuffie leaned on the far other side, overlooking the town. "Ben McGuffie? We need to talk to you."

He flicked off his radio and spun on his heel. His face flushed and contorted. "Who are you?"

"McCain County Sheriff's Department," Doak said pointing to his badge. "We want to ask you a couple of questions."

"Starting with what you're doing on the roof."

McDuffie tugged his cowboy hat over his eyes and closed the gap between us. "I'm studying the weather. I fancy myself an amateur meteorologist."

The answer was smooth and quick but I didn't buy it. "And what are you doing with a police scanner?"

"I use it to pick up the weather reports." He pointed to the radio. "I'm a bit of a pluviophiles, a lover of the weather."

"Is the storm letting up any time soon?" I asked.

"Not with the low-pressure front comin' from the north. Afraid we're in for a long, wet night."

The only problem with asking the question was I didn't know enough about the weather to call his bluff. His assessment could be nonsense but I couldn't tell.

"What is it you folks are after?" McDuffie asked. "Am I breaking some sort of law being up here?"

"You're trespassing on private property," Doak said. "And we aren't taking any chances after the fire on the diner's roof."

I cocked my head to the side. "Do you know anything about it?"

"The fire?" His lips pursed. "Well, I'm not sure it's my place to say but I noticed a woman carrying a can of gasoline about an hour before the blaze."

"Really?"

He nodded. "Yes, ma'am. Now maybe she was just fillin' up her lawn mower but that sight's been botherin' me the last few hours. She looked innocent enough and smiled as I passed by. But when I asked if she was havin' car trouble and needed help, she ran off."

"Could you identify the woman if you saw her again?" Doak asked.

"I think she might be related to the fella who owns the bookstore." He removed his cowboy hat and scrubbed a hand through damp hair. "You don't think the fire is connected to the missing book, do ya?"

I raised an eyebrow. "Mr. McDuffie, we heard you tried to purchase the journal yesterday but were turned down flat. You don't strike me as the type of guy who takes no for an answer."

"Perhaps you should talk to the woman with the gas can. If someone started the fire, she's a good place to start." He pivoted to Doak. "Don't you agree, Deputy?"

"I... we don't think you saw Christy or anyone else set the fire."

I nodded. "We think you took the pilgrim journal, McDuffie."

"Me?" He pointed to his chest. "If I was a thief, why would I still be here instead of running to Mexico with my booty?"

"Because you thought your hero show would avert suspicion," I said.

"Speaking of heroics." A half smile danced across his face. "About two dozen people will confirm I was nowhere near the bookstore when the treasure disappeared. You ought to check your facts, detective."

I had no proof against him. No evidence except my gut. But something told me he was guilty. Innocent people weren't so smug. And they didn't rehearse their answers. "I know you did it, McDuffie. I'm just working on the how."

He laughed. "You're confident but you're dead wrong. I can't be in two places at once, now can I?"

"Maybe you had an accomplice or maybe you did some sort of magic trick misdirection." I pointed my finger at him. "But I'm going to prove what you did."

He snatched my wrist and squeezed. "I invite you to try, little lady." His friendly smile turned sinister and chills raced across my spine.

Doak landed a strong right hook into McDuffie's jaw and sent his black cowboy hat rolling across the roof. "You're under arrest for assault."

"I think you got that backward, Son. You're the one who sucker punched me." McDuffie spit blood. "I could have your badge."

Doak didn't back down and used his height to tower over the troubadour. "You don't touch her again, you hear me?"

He retrieved his muddy hat and whistled a tune. "Hope to see you folks at the show. It's gonna be unforgettable." He winked as he climbed down the ladder.

"Your arm okay?" Doak asked.

"Fine." I rubbed the red skin. "Worth the bruise because I got him to crack. He has a bad temper."

"You shouldn't purposely provoke bad guys, Lizzie."

"I wasn't worried with a halfway-decent cowboy as backup."

Doak rifled a hand through his thick hair. "How do we go about finding evidence?"

"We need to find his accomplice. But I have no idea who might be helping him." I sighed. "And I don't care what he said about the 'weather radar', he's listening to the police scanner."

Doak touched the receiver attached to his shoulder. "Which means we ought to stay off the radio until we identify who's helping him."

# Chapter 7
# Needle in a Haystack
## Samantha

Becky attempted to remove her pilgrim bonnet out of frustration but struggled with the knot under her chin. She yanked and tugged but it wouldn't budge. "Is this thing stapled to my head?"

I pulled one side of the ribbon and the knot released. "Try and stay calm, Beckers."

"I'm calm as cucumber... cool as? Which is it?"

"Doesn't matter because you're neither."

"I am too."

"You're so nervous your hands are shaking."

She glared at her orange nail polish. "I'm as steady as a surgeon. What would I have to be nervous about? We've done way more dangerous stuff than this."

"My thoughts exactly."

"Except this time we sent Lizzie to interview a rambler who turned out to be a thief by herself."

I shook my head and held open the door to the Royal Crown Theater. "We have no proof McDuffie is the thief. All we know is he made an offer to buy the journal."

"Lizzie left to interview him an hour ago, never returned, and isn't answering our calls."

"She's probably busy."

Becky pocketed her phone. "And now Boone isn't answering. Why is everyone we know disappearing? This is like a horror movie."

I caught a glimpse of the football game on someone's phone screen. "And to top it off, the Cowboys are losing."

"To RGIII and the Redskins?" Becky rolled her eyes. "Romo better get it together."

We navigated backstage and I grabbed a pilgrim by the arm. "We're looking for McDuffie, is he here?"

The pilgrim checked his digital watch. "Yeah, but he's going on in ten."

"Where is he?"

"Dressing room."

Becky led the way to the movie theater's supply closet serving as a makeshift dressing room. She knocked on the door. "Mr. McDuffie?"

The door swung open and McDuffie snagged his cowboy hat from the coat rack. "Is it time already?"

"No, you still have a little bit."

I stepped in front of Becky. "Can we ask you a few questions?"

"About?"

"The missing pilgrim journal," I said. "We're helping the sheriff's department interview witnesses."

He adjusted the collar of his three-quarter zip sweater. "I'm happy to help in any way I can."

I flipped through my blank notebook. "I apologize if you already answered these questions in your previous interview."

"No one's talked to me yet."

I shared a look with Becky. "My sister didn't stop by to speak to you?"

McDuffie shook his head. "I don't think so. What does she look like?"

"Like Samantha," Becky said. "They're identical twins."

"Then definitely not." He chuckled. "I think I would have remembered the déjà vu."

My pulse raced but I ignored the fear and focused on the job in front of me. Just because Lizzie never showed up for the interview didn't mean something happened to her. I cleared my throat and started asking McDuffie basic witness questions – the boring unassuming things that established a rhythm. If I jumped right in with an accusation, he'd shut down.

He checked the time. "Does that about do it?"

"Almost." Becky jotted a note. "We just have a few loose ends to tie up for the report."

I drummed my pen on the pad. "The sheriffs are particular about loose ends. A case can't be closed if they both aren't satisfied."

"I understand but unfortunately I'm running out of time."

"Just a quick second... ugh, where is it?" I thumbed through the notebook, pretending to search through interview notes. "Here we go. Christy Watkins mentioned you made an offer to purchase the pilgrim journal."

"I did." He reached for his guitar and strummed the strings with an open palm. He twisted the knob and tuned the instrument. "She and her brother turned me down flat."

"Why did you want it?" Becky asked. "There can't be much of a profit in buying and flipping it."

"No probably not." He chuckled. "I recently did one of those DNA tests and found out I had ancestors on the Mayflower."

I shrugged. "You and about thirty-five million people."

He fiddled with the strings until they were in tune. "You make an excellent point. The lineage isn't exactly rare. But after intense Googling, I discovered my family was mentioned in Henry Samson's journal. I wanted to buy it as a gift. It would mean a heck of a lot to my Pappy. More than the professor who bought it at auction to look smart in front of his fancy friends."

"Were you irritated Dr. Watkins wouldn't sell?" I asked.

"I might have been a little miffed but hey, I get it. He spent a lot of money to add the treasure to his collection and gigs like this one don't pay me near enough to make a competitive offer." He twirled a guitar pick through his fingers. "But you miss a hundred percent of the shots you don't take, right?"

"I don't mean to offend you, Mr. McDuffie, but that gives you substantial motive to steal the journal," I said.

"It probably does." He placed his guitar in the case. "But the good news is I have a solid alibi – fightin' off that fire."

"Can you think of anyone who might have looked suspicious?" Becky asked. "Someone who wasn't around during the fire?"

His finger drummed over his mouth. "You know, I don't know if this means anything but I saw Miss Christy carrying a can of gasoline. Now I'm not sayin' she started the fire but it was mighty odd."

I shut my notebook. "Thanks, Mr. McDuffie. We appreciate your time."

"Sure thing."

"Have a terrific show," Becky said as she closed the dressing room door. She twirled into me. "Okay, so where's Lizzie?"

I fished my iPhone out of my back pocket and activated the app to locate her phone. "We're about to find out."

Becky drummed her sneaker on the carpeted floor of the movie theater. "What's the holdup?"

"It claims Lizzie's across the street." We followed the GPS outside and I pointed toward the pharmacy. I spotted my sister with our former ranch hand, Doak Walker Montgomery. "There."

Becky ran to Lizzie and her giant bear hug almost knocked them both over. "You're alive."

Lizzie's brows knit together. "Was there doubt?"

"Why didn't you answer your phone?" I asked.

She glanced at Doak and shrugged. "We've been busy. We just interviewed McDuffie and boy does he have a temper."

"He was calm during our interview." I frowned. "And he specifically said he never spoke to you."

"He lied." She held up her bruised wrist. "Doak gave him a bloody lip."

Becky's eyes widened. "The guy must have excellent stage makeup."

I crossed my arms. "Obviously, you're still stuck on the McDuffie is guilty theory."

Lizzie mirrored my posture. "And obviously you're still skeptical."

"The police can't make an arrest based on your gut." I gestured to her hand. "And confronting him didn't work out so well."

"What exactly did McDuffie say in your interview?" Becky asked.

"He invited us to prove it." Doak tossed his broad shoulders. "Innocent people don't behave like him."

"We agree but…"

Lizzie flung her arms. "Always a but with you."

"He has an alibi for the switch so there must be an accomplice," I said.

"Unless our timeline is off."

My gaze darted to Becky. "I can't see how. Gobbles was pardoned and appeared in the case after the fire. That's the only possible window."

"I guess."

"When you talked to McDuffie, did he shift the blame onto Christy?" Lizzie asked.

I nodded. "But we don't think she's involved."

"Are you sure?" Doak asked. "Because they could point fingers at each other to throw us off."

"Absolutely." Becky leaned against the park bench. "At first we thought she was fleeing town because she was packing up a taxi and it turned out she was but…"

"Christy is a mess. She couldn't pull off a heist," I said.

Lizzie sighed. "Where does that leave us on the partner front?"

"I know who did it!" Boone Hitchcock raced across the Circle, carrying Gobbles in his arms like an oversized football. "Guys, I know who did it."

My forehead wrinkled. "How?"

"The feed store angle." He shoved a receipt at me. "Dylan Fulbright."

Lizzie gritted her teeth. "Ivy League."

# Chapter 8
# Double Trouble
## Lizzie

Darkness fell upon the Circle as the hour approached six o'clock. The drizzle finally relented and a crowd flocked to town for the Pilgrim Pageant. With the sudden influx of looky-loos, we moved our sleuth meeting inside the *Lake Falls Gazette*.

Samantha twirled the key around her forefinger. "What makes you think Dylan Fulbright is the accomplice?"

"Didn't you read the feed store receipt?" Boone removed his tall hat and ruffled his hair. "The proof is right there in black and white."

"Good enough for me." I grinned. "I'd love to see that smug brat behind bars."

"Plenty of people purchase feed but it doesn't make him an accomplice," Samantha said. "We need to prove a connection between Dylan and McDuffie."

"I figured you would say that." Boone scrolled through pictures on his phone. "I caught Dylan rummaging through the first aid section of the pharmacy. Notice the burns on his arms... war wounds from arson I imagine."

Becky high-fived him. "This is huge."

"That's why McDuffie was on the roof of the pharmacy," I said. "He was meeting with his accomplice."

Doak lifted his cowboy hat and rubbed his forehead. "What's the motive? What does he need the money for? He's a snobby rich kid."

"Or is he?" I asked.

"That's an interesting question you pose." Samantha leaned on the edge of a desk. "Grifters often work in pairs. One person comes to town early to establish a rapport with locals and lay a foundation. Then they set up the con for their accomplice."

"Ivy League has been here three months and he's already weaseled his way onto the party planning committee," I said.

Becky snapped her fingers. "Dylan is the one who recommended McDuffie for the show."

"I thought he answered an ad," Doak said.

"Not exactly." Becky shook her head. "I caught up on my gossip since my train arrived. The performers who responded to the ad were more of the boring performance art types from last year. They were desperate for anything else when Dylan showed them a DVD of McDuffie. I'm not sure how he found him."

I raised an eyebrow. "Well, that's certainly suspicious."

"Where can we find Dylan?" Samantha asked.

Becky craned her neck to check my watch. "The Pilgrim Pageant is about to start. He's playing John Smith."

While the theater director ushered Boone and Becky to their marks, Samantha, Doak, and I snuck backstage to locate the accomplice.

I gritted my teeth as I locked eyes with Ivy League. Not only was he rude and arrogant, but he was also a criminal to boot. "We need a word, Dylan."

"I think I can spare a moment for my biggest fans." He stroked his hair, thinking it looked cool. "Want my autograph, ladies?"

"Only if it comes with your written confession," I said.

"Confession?" He jerked his chin. "Is that why Lurch is here?"

Samantha grabbed his arm. "Lift your sleeve."

"I always knew you were the one sweet on me."

"Enough with the comedy act." She poked the gauze wrapped around his forearm. "Explain how you got these burns."

"No need to be rough. I'm happy to explain." He winced. "But not in front of the deputy. Four's a crowd."

Doak placed his hands on his hips and hovered over the smaller guy. "Looks to me like your little arson plan backfired."

"Arson?" Dylan snorted. "Bro, this is from trying to deep fry a turkey with frat guys... who may or may not have been inebriated."

"We know about the con," I said. "You arrived in town first to scope things out and select a mark for McDuffie."

"You're pretty Brown, but you're crazy." He grinned. "Which isn't a dealbreaker, by the way."

"The sheriffs are arresting your partner as we speak." Samantha edged closer. "Do you honestly think he won't roll on you if given the chance?"

His eyes darted between us. "I don't have any idea what you guys are talking about. What are you accusing me of?"

"Stealing the pilgrim journal," Doak said.

"Ah, thanks for catching me up." Dylan slapped his shoulder. "I have enough money in my monthly allowance to buy four of those. Why would I steal it?"

"Because you aren't a rich trust fund snob." I shrugged. "Just a snob."

"I'm all that and more. Look at my platinum credit cards." He opened his wallet. "Call up any country club in Connecticut and they'll know the Fulbrights. Better yet call any boarding school on the East Coast. I was kicked out of all of them."

"And that's supposed to convince us you aren't a criminal?" Samantha asked.

"It's supposed to convince you I'm rich. I don't need some stupid old book and I certainly wouldn't team up with that hick McDuffie."

"You recommended him for the show," Doak said. "Explain how you knew him."

"I didn't. I saw his name on Mrs. Parker's short list of candidates and I was sucking up. It's what I do best."

"Stop lying, Ivy League." I pinched the bridge of my nose. I wanted him to be guilty so badly I wasn't thinking objectively.

"I'm hurt, Brown. Wounded." He spread his arms. "The good news is you guys have got squat for proof."

Samantha narrowed her gaze. "Where were you during the fire? Just after Gobbles was pardoned."

"After you and your boyfriend ran me off? I met my buddies for deep-fried turkey."

Samantha frowned. "Boyfriend?"

"He's talking about me and Boone," I said.

He pointed. "You're Lizzie. I can never tell you apart."

"Since when are you dating Boone?" Doak asked.

"I'm not."

Doak's brows knit together. "Samantha is?"

"Definitely not." Her nose scrunched. "I can't stand his magic tricks."

"They aren't so bad…"

Dylan waved. "See, this is my problem. You guys are identical and I can't keep up. I don't see why that makes me the bad guy."

"Their personalities are completely different." Doak tipped his cowboy hat. "Anyone who takes the time to get to know them sees the subtle differences. Even when they swap places. Lizzie is sarcastic and gets a sparkle in her eye when she's about to land a zinger. Samantha's brilliant and she'd rather spend her afternoon with a dog or horse than most people."

"Same hair, same eyes, same size." Dylan shrugged. "They wear different clothes but other than that, they probably can read each other's mind."

I twirled to my twin sister. "Samantha!"

"What?"

"Even identical twins have vastly different personalities." She nodded. "I'm aware."

"One might be friendly and personable while the other has a short fuse."

"Two places at once." Her back straightened. "McDuffie didn't have an accomplice. Or at least not in the way we thought."

A smile spread across my face. "He's a twin."

# Chapter 9
# Turkey Trot
## Samantha

The choir busted into song, drowning out my thoughts. My forehead creased as I backed further away from the curtain. McDuffie was a twin. The solution was so simple and Lizzie and I missed it.

"Ironic, I know." Lizzie offered a sheepish shrug as she brought the rest of the team up to speed.

"Are you sure?" Boone asked. "There are two McDuffies?"

"It would explain why Doak gave the evil twin a bloody lip and the one in his dressing room seems fine." Becky pointed a thumb over her shoulder. "No amount of makeup fixes a fat lip."

"Or how he was dry two minutes after standing in the rain with us." Lizzie spread her arms. "We are certain about the twin angle but we're still lacking in the proof department."

"We need to draw them out," I said. "One of the twins must have the journal."

"Probably the guy on the roof." Doak rubbed his chin. "He's the behind-the-scenes twin, keeping an eye on the cops with his scanner."

Lizzie snapped her fingers. "And I know just how we catch him."

"How?" Becky asked.

"We're going to require a little help from the co-sheriffs and Dr. Watkins."

I checked the time. "We better organize this quick. McDuffie goes on after the choir and something tells me he'll disappear following his set."

"That gives us forty-five minutes." Lizzie tossed her shoulders. "Plenty of time."

Lizzie and I hustled across the street to the police station and busted into the interview room where the co-sheriffs took a run at Christy.

"Excuse you." Durwood lurched from his seat. "We're a little busy in here. No room for the Hardy Girls."

"We know who stole the pilgrim journal," I said. "And it wasn't her."

Andi placed her hands on her hips. "Who was it?"

"McDuffie," Lizzie said.

Durwood's head dropped to the tabletop. "What part of A-L-I-B-I don't you understand?"

"Ben McDuffie has an identical twin." Lizzie grinned. "Which makes his A-L-I-B-I moot."

"And you know this how?" Durwood asked.

"It's a twin thing," Lizzie and I said in unison. We didn't believe in the twins reading each other's mind nonsense but it was a much quicker and believable explanation for him to swallow.

"Do you have any proof?" Andi asked.

"That's why we're here." I cleared my throat. "We have a plan to catch the McDuffie twins but we need help."

"They're keeping tabs on the investigation via a police scanner," Lizzie said. "They know you brought in Dr. Watkins and now his sister. We can use that knowledge to our advantage."

"We're the sheriff's department." Durwood shook his head. "We don't resort to cheap tricks like some alphabet organization TV show."

"The only reason you're a co-sheriff is because you helped Samantha and Lizzie with a 4th of July scheme." Andi rolled her eyes. "What do y'all have in mind?"

"We lean into the insurance fraud theory." Lizzie pursed her lips. "Y'all announce over the radio you're arresting Dr. Watkins for insurance fraud following the Pilgrim Pageant. He made a phony copy of the journal and the real one is hidden in the bookstore."

"Then you tell Doak to pick up the real one from the safe and bring it to the police station," I said.

Durwood's bushy brows knit together. "Why? What is all this going to accomplish?"

"It's going to draw McDuffie 2 out of hiding and force him to break into the Wordsmith." Lizzie leaned on the edge of the table. "He won't be able to resist."

Andi brushed curls over her shoulder. "What if he doesn't fall for it?"

"Or what if only one twin goes for it?" Durwood asked.

I shrugged. "We only need one."

"If we time this out right, McDuffie 1 will be on stage, forcing McDuffie 2 out of the shadows."

"We're fairly certain McDuffie 2 is in possession of the journal. So, when he breaks into the bookstore you'll get him for B&E and the original crime."

Andi turned to her co-sheriff. "What do you think?"

"This is never going to work." Durwood stroked his mustache. "We can't con a con."

Christy raised her hand. "I don't know if I'm allowed a vote but I like it."

I grinned. "The ayes have it. You've been outvoted, Durwood."

"We want to help." Becky's bonnet fell below her eyes. "Don't stick us on the bench."

"You are helping by watching this McDuffie." I gestured to the stage as the troubadour grabbed his guitar. "For this to work, we don't want any surprises."

"I get the feeling you want us out of the way." Boone adjusted his glasses. "Sort of like the wild turkey chase you sent me on at the feed store."

"You insisted it would pan out."

"You never even asked Dylan Fulbright why he bought turkey feed."

"Probably for Gobble's pardoning," Becky whispered. "He's party planning committee, remember?"

"Anyway, can y'all handle watching McDuffie?"

Becky smiled. "You got it, boss."

"Don't feel too bad, the co-sheriffs are sticking us on the bench too." Lizzie buttoned her peacoat. "We get to watch the action unfold from the park."

"That's great." Becky twisted her mouth. "Well, not great but I'm glad we're in the same boat."

Doak flashed a thumbs up from the wings of the stage and I nodded. "The sheriffs just made the announcement. We better get in position."

Lizzie and I exited through the back door and circled the alley. "Keep your eyes peeled," she said.

"As opposed to what?"

"I don't know, it's just something people say. I'm making conversation."

"Not every moment of silence needs to be filled." I took a seat on the park bench. "I'll watch the north."

"That goes without saying." She plopped on the other side of the bench, facing the opposite direction. "Durwood is exiting the movie theater with Dr. Watkins."

The professor hollered all the way to the station. I pulled my knit cap over my ears. "Is he that good of an actor or did we forget to fill him in on the plan?"

Lizzie shifted for a better view of the Wordsmith. "How long do you think McDuffie 2 will wait to make his move?"

"He'll want to act before Doak retrieves the journal." I cocked my head to the side. "Assuming he's listening to the scanner and buys our ruse."

"He is definitely listening. And I hope he takes the bait. You realize I'm staking my reputation on this."

"We all are."

"Yeah, but it's my job on the line."

"The professor would be stupid to fire you. If it wasn't for us, he'd never see the pilgrim journal again."

"He still might not if the plan fails."

"Have a little faith, Lizzie." I pointed a gloved hand to the pharmacy's fire escape. A shadow wearing a cowboy hat dropped to the ground. "He's on the move."

She released a dramatic sigh. "Thank goodness." Her voice squeaked as the shadow turned in the opposite direction of the bookstore. "Hey, where is he going?"

"Maybe he's circling the store to make sure he isn't being followed."

"Or he saw through our con and isn't coming." She sprung from the bench.

"Where are you going?"

"We can't lose him."

"We're supposed to stay out of the way."

She rolled her eyes. "Since when do we listen to authority figures?"

"Now might be a good time to start seeing as the plan hinges on McDuffie not noticing us."

"If he's fleeing, we're the only ones who can follow him." She pointed. "Andi is in the bookstore, Durwood is at the station, and Doak is in the theater. We're the last defense."

"You're being dramatic. McDuffie isn't leaving his brother."

"Not all twins are best friends like us. McDuffie 2 is cold and evil. Maybe he doesn't care what happens to McDuffie 1."

"We really need to learn their first names."

Lizzie waved me over. "Are you coming?"

"Someone's gotta have your back."

We jogged across the Circle and peeked around the pharmacy. McDuffie looked over his shoulder and dropped to the wet ground. He stretched for something underneath the dumpster.

"What is he doing?" Lizzie asked.

I forced my eyes to focus despite the darkness. He retrieved something rectangular shaped encased in a plastic baggy. "That might be the pilgrim journal."

"Might be? What else would he take the time to hide under a dumpster?"

"It's only a theory. I can't confirm from this distance."

Lizzie grabbed my arm. "Come on, he's on the move again."

"Perhaps he'll go to the Wordsmith now."

He turned to the left and hit the sidewalk in a dead sprint. Lizzie took off after him. "Which is why he's bolting in the opposite direction of Main Street?"

"Alright, maybe he's running."

McDuffie disappeared behind the post office and headed for the parking lot. If he had a getaway car waiting, we were in trouble.

Lizzie glanced over her shoulder, sharing my concern. "I think it's time we call the sheriffs."

I slowed my pace and fished my phone out of my pocket. "I'll make the call."

She continued to pursue the perp. "I'll try to get a license plate." She screamed and her furry boots left the ground.

"Lizzie?"

She moaned as a gloved hand covered her mouth. Her arms and legs flailed as McDuffie carried her toward a fire engine red convertible. One thing was certain, it wasn't the type of car for blending in.

"Don't come any closer." He flashed a small snake gun, a .22 by the looks of it. "I wonder if the old wives' tale about a twin feeling each other's pain is true. Might be fun to experiment."

"Allow me." Lizzie kicked his shin but McDuffie didn't release her.

He pulled back the hammer. "Don't test me. I can shoot you and use your sister as a hostage."

"What do you need a hostage for?" she mumbled.

"I think I ferreted out your little con but in case I'm wrong and the coppers set up a roadblock, I have you as leverage." An edge filled his once musical South Carolina accent.

"What about your brother?" I asked. "You're just going to leave him?"

"With me and the journal out of the picture, y'all got nothin' on old Franklin."

Lizzie snorted. "Ben and Franklin. How patriotic."

"Get in the car and be quiet." He opened the driver's side door and shoved Lizzie inside. "I'll let her go when I'm a safe distance out of town. As long as I don't spot any smokies following me. Am I clear?"

I nodded and focused my attention on Lizzie. I couldn't trust McDuffie to let her go which meant I couldn't let him escape. But how did I get around the gun issue and the car issue? Would I have time to get to my truck? Could I get close enough before he spotted me? I needed more time to make a plan and somehow relay it to Lizzie. But how?

She bobbed her head. "Stephenville."

*What?* I shook my head, unsure what she meant.

"No talking," McDuffie said as he opened the rear door.

Lizzie pressed a button and lowered the convertible's top.

"What are you doing?" McDuffie climbed in the backseat behind the driver's side. "Stop pressing buttons and put the top up."

"It's stuck," Lizzie said.

He reached over her and started the engine, the gun remained trained on her as they pulled out of the lot and drove east. The taillights weren't yet out of sight when I sprinted to the other direction. We parked the truck a mile away on the opposite end of Main Street. I didn't have time to waste.

A motorcycle slowed to the sidewalk and revved. Dylan raised his visor and killed the engine. "If you're coming to apologize, you're too late."

I skidded to a stop. "I need to borrow your motorcycle."

"I can't stay mad. You're too cute." He tossed me his extra helmet. "I can give you a ride. Maybe cruise down to the lake."

I shook my hair free and struggled to make the helmet fit comfortably. "This is an emergency."

"I knew you would come around. We're two kindred spirits, Brown." He winked. "Make sure to hold on tight to me. I drive fast."

"Lizzie's in trouble I don't have time for this." I shoved him off the bike and he sailed into the bushes.

I grabbed the clutch and climbed on the lime-green Ninja. I started the engine and stepped down into first gear.

Dylan plopped up from the shrubs with leaves in his hair. "Hey! That's my bike."

"Sorry." I released the clutch and the motorcycle eased away from the curb. He stumbled to his feet and ran after me. I pulled back on the throttle to give it a little speed. "I'll bring it back in one piece."

Rather than dwelling on whether Dylan would have me arrested, I focused on Lizzie's coded message. What did she mean by Stephenville? Could she be referring to the rodeo?

Unlike me, Lizzie wasn't an avid rider and she seldom competed. But at the Stephenville Rodeo, her competitiveness got the best of her and we entered as an amateur trick-riding pair. Our trick was Lizzie escaping from an out-of-control stagecoach and bailing onto my horse. All while traveling at top speeds. We practiced for months and earned the blue ribbon. Executing the trick with a convertible and a motorcycle was considerably harder but not impossible.

But first I had to catch her. I focused on the pitch-black stretch in front of me, thankful I knew the roads by memory. A cloudy night in the country made visibility terrible even with the high beams on.

I eased off the throttle as taillights glowed red a quarter mile ahead of me. It was dangerous to cut my lights but more dangerous to Lizzie if I didn't.

"You know these roads better than him," I whispered to myself.

Knowing we needed to make our move before the bridge, I increased my speed. When I was within striking distance, I flicked my passing lights. Lizzie double-tapped her brakes.

The shadowy figure of McDuffie turned around in his rear seat and hollered. He fired the .22 in my direction but I didn't flinch. Beyond two or three feet that particular snake gun was practically useless.

Lizzie jerked the lever on her manual seat, leaned it back, and rammed it into McDuffie. His gun sparked as it clattered to the highway. He struggled from under the seat and grabbed at Lizzie's neck. She managed to fight him off but his strength would eventually win out. She slowed the convertible and again shoved the seat, incapacitating McDuffie.

I pulled alongside the cruising vehicle and before we could debate a better course, she hopped onto the back of the bike. Just like the rodeo trick we practiced a thousand times.

Though we were only going about thirty by the time we made the switch, my heart raced like we were going one hundred.

I eased on both the foot and hand brakes while the convertible sailed over the bridge and continued to the lake with a splash.

Lizzie hobbled off the bike. "Call the sheriffs."

"Where are you going?"

"Fishing."

"For McDuffie or the journal?" I hit the engine kill switch and followed her.

"Both, I guess." She kicked off her furry boots. "I'm a lifeguard. I can't let him drown even if he did try to kill me."

"Do you realize how cold the water is? I'd rather roll the dice that he can swim."

"Samantha!"

I kicked off my cowboy boots and removed my jacket. "Fine, I'll help you save the evil twin."

"It's the season of thanks after all. Maybe he'll be grateful."

"Grateful we drove his car off a bridge?" I grabbed a sturdy stick from the shore. "Just in case he isn't."

"Good call." She waded into the water and her voice rose an octave. "That'll wake you up."

Before the water reached my calves, she power stroked to the middle of the lake. The car started to sink and there was still no sign of McDuffie. Lizzie ducked below the surface and stayed under for nearly a minute. My frozen limbs cut through the icy lake as I carefully made my way to help.

She pierced through the water, her arms underneath McDuffie. He sported a large gash on his forehead. "He was thrown from the car and hit his head."

"Prime example of why you should always wear your seatbelt." I slung his other arm over my shoulder and helped her drag him to shore.

"Is it me or does it seem like a lot of our cases end with a chase into the lake?"

I shrugged. "We do live in Lake Falls."

"Place him down on his back." Lizzie hovered over him and checked his breathing. She interlocked her fingers and started chest compressions.

McDuffie rolled over and coughed up water.

Red and blue lights flashed in the distance and Doak's police SUV drove straight up the beach. He spilled out with Becky and Boone.

"How did y'all find us?" I asked.

"Dylan reported his bike stolen." Doak slid beside us and cuffed McDuffie. "Is he okay?"

"Groggy. Probably needs a doctor to look at his head." Lizzie removed a sealed plastic bag from the waistband of her jeans. "Found this on him."

"You got the pilgrim journal." I smiled. "That's why you were under for so long."

"I guess this means we have plenty of evidence to arrest these guys," Becky said.

"We can add kidnapping and reckless discharge of a firearm to his long list of offenses." Lizzie massaged the back of her neck. "And anything else we can tack on."

Boone grabbed a wool blanket from the cruiser and wrapped it around Lizzie's shoulders. "You must be freezing. We have the heat on in the truck so you can warm up."

"Don't worry about me. I'm fine." I rolled my eyes. "Hardly even wet."

Becky handed me the coat I tossed onto the bank. "Could he be any more obvious?"

"He's as obvious as she is oblivious." I slipped my arms into my jacket and shivered. "This was a Thanksgiving we'll never forget."

"You can say that again." Doak slammed the backdoor of his cruiser. "The co-sheriffs just arrested the other McDuffie."

"Franklin," I said. "The evil one here is Ben."

"The other one might be friendlier but they're both conmen who tried to ruin Thanksgiving." Becky frowned at the SUV. "How are all of us supposed to fit with the criminal."

I lifted Dylan's motorcycle out of the mud. "Hop on, Beckers."

"I'd rather ride a horse."

# Chapter 10
## Give Thanks
### Lizzie

All at once I was overcome by exhaustion and hunger and I couldn't tell which was in the lead. My stomach gurgled like a grizzly bear and I found it difficult to keep my eyes open. But somehow, I managed to make my official statement for the co-sheriffs.

"I can't believe Dr. Watkins didn't thank us," Becky said as we pulled up to the Twin Bluebonnet Ranch. "I didn't expect a Macy's parade but a simple job well done would have been nice."

"At least he didn't fire me."

"He acted like we ruined his Thanksgiving."

"Speaking of ruined plans, are you sure I'm not intruding?" Becky asked. "It's late and there might not be enough food. Or worse, your folks might be sleeping."

My eyes darted to the dashboard clock – ten 'til midnight. "I bet everyone's headed to the Heartland Mall for Black Friday."

"I'm not sad to miss that." Samantha parked underneath the carport and cut the engine. "I'd much rather skip the line and shop Cyber Monday."

Becky shifted on the truck's bench seat. "Is that your brother outside?"

"Since when does he do chores this late?" Samantha asked.

"Since when does he do chores?" I corrected. Since moving out and joining the fast track to the Texas Rangers police, our older brother left ranch management to us.

"He's replacing a window," Samantha said.

I chuckled and jogged across the lawn. "Guess this means the Cowboys lost?"

Wil smiled, producing dimples. "I don't want to talk about it."

"What did you throw, the remote?"

His mouth twitched. "My boot."

"You took your boot off and hurled it through the window?" I arched a brow. "This is why people gossip about the famous Brown temper."

"They lost to the Redskins, Lizzie. The Redskins. They stink."

Samantha huffed. "I'm almost glad we missed the game."

"They would have won if I was watching and wearing my good luck Romo jersey," I said.

"What you wear while watching a game has nothing to do with the outcome on the field," Samantha said.

"And yet they always win for me."

"I sure hope there are leftovers." She walked away from me and scooted into the house to greet our Dalmatian, Whodunit.

Becky waved goodbye to Wil and followed us inside. "Did anyone ever mention he resembles Superman… well the *Smallville* version which technically isn't Superman."

"You've mentioned it once or twice, Beckaroo."

Samantha retrieved plates from the cabinet and plastic-covered casserole dishes from the fridge. "I didn't realize how hungry I was until I smelled Mom's mac and cheese."

I grabbed a turkey leg from the fridge and bit into it. Whodunit stood on her back legs and I tossed her a piece. "I say we start with dessert because we don't have to wait for the microwave."

Becky cut a slice of blueberry pie. "I know it's kinda corny but before we eat my family always says what they're thankful for. Do y'all mind?"

"Go for it." Samantha stole the turkey leg and took a giant bite.

"I'm thankful y'all invited me home from college. Especially since my mom was away on a business trip. I couldn't spend another minute with my annoying roommate. Lois has never even seen *Gilmore Girls* and she claims to be a TV fan."

"Nice one." I gave her a thumbs up. "Not too sappy and just the right amount of complaining."

"Now y'all go."

"I'm thankful I made my Army Pie yesterday because I never would have found the time today." I shoveled a sizeable piece of flaky crust, sweet berries, and Bluebell ice cream onto my fork. "What about you, Samantha?"

"I'm thankful Mom baked a ham." Samantha scrunched her nose. "Because turkey is terrible and dry. Why did it become the definitive Thanksgiving food?"

I threw my arm around her shoulders. "Just when I was starting to think we didn't share that supernatural twin thing, you read my mind."

"Also, while we're at it, can we stop with the green bean casserole?" Becky asked. "It's always half molten lava half frozen and then has the gross onion toppings. No thanks."

I gasped. "Now that is just un–American. If not for the green bean casserole, dogs everywhere wouldn't get sneaky table scraps. Yams would move down the list and become the most hated dish. Because let's face it, the only thing keeping it from being dead last are the tiny marshmallows."

Samantha's brows arched. "What does that leave us with? Mac and cheese, rolls, and creamed corn?"

"And room for dessert." I held out my empty plate. "Pass the delicious brownie pie, please."

## Quick Author's Note

Happy Thanksgiving y'all!

Thank you for reading Turkey, Thievery, and Twins. I hope you loved it. One of my favorite cozy mystery themes is holidays and in a quirky town like Lake Falls, anything can happen! From the Pilgrim Pageant to the pardoning of Gobbles, the residents stay pretty busy.

Up next in the series is Sleuths, Sabotage and Sandcastles. The co-sheriffs make another appearance as they campaign for the special election and fans of my Hollywood Whodunit series will enjoy a familiar character in Gallagher Robinson. Keep reading to find out more.

Collect all the Twin Bluebonnet Ranch Mysteries!

# A free book for you...

**All caught up? Just getting started?**
  Whether you're a super fan or a newbie to the Lake Falls universe, join my newsletter for an exclusive bonus story you won't find anywhere else! Seven beloved characters, four charming eras, one puzzling mystery. Download your FREE copy of *The Secret of the Bluebonnet Ranch* today.

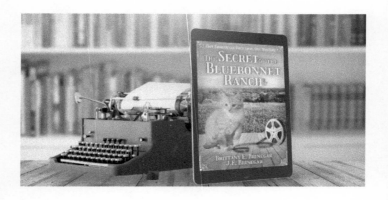

**Some people inherit antiques, but these sleuths inherit a whodunit spanning decades.**

Get ready for an epic crossover cozy mystery, where four dynamic heroines from different eras unite to solve a hand-me-down case involving a mysterious pendant and a secret legend lurking below the surface of a small Texas town.

Penelope, the daring flapper of 1924.
Jenny, the silver-tongued post-war investigator of 1949.
Samantha, the tech-savvy sleuth of 2012.
Becky, the nosy actress of modern day.

Join these remarkable women as they employ wit, charm, and intelligence to unravel a web of secrets passed down through the ages. A thrilling read for cozy mystery enthusiasts and history buffs alike!

https://www.brittanybrinegar.com/subscribe

# Next in the Series

The last thing Lizzie Brown wants to do on the 104-degree August day is participate in the Sandcastle Showdown. But thanks to her overly competitive twin sister, they're challenging the four-time champ.

When the eccentric inventor vanishes before defending his crown, everyone brushes it off – except the twins. A cryptic phone call sparks their suspicion of foul play, propelling them into a search for their toughest competitor. Can the twins beat the heat and uncover the truth in time?

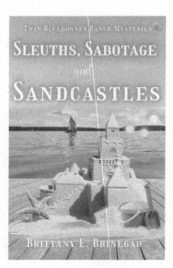

Order Now

# About the Author

**Brittany E. Brinegar** is the author of witty mysteries and whodunits. When you open one of her books, look out for rapid-fire banter and nostalgic pop culture references.

Her hobbies include time travel to the 1940s, solving mysteries, and training to be a super spy... vicariously through her characters of course.

She lives in Arlington, Texas with two canine writing companions/distractions and loves drawing inspiration from family, friends, and her home state.

Ready to smile your way through murder? Join Brittany's newsletter and never miss a new release.

Website: https://www.brittanybrinegar.com/

# Books by Britt

## Hollywood Whodunit

*A Humorous Cozy Mystery*

Prime Time Murder (Book 1)

Stand-In Murder (Book 2)

Music City Murder (Book 3)

Trap Door Murder (Book 4)

Fool's Gold Murder (Book 5)

Holly Jolly Murder (Book 6)

Blue Suede Murder (Book 7)

Family Reunion Murder (Book 8)

Summer Vacation Murder (Book 9)

Sunlight Swindler Murder (Book 10)

## Spies of Texas

*A Witty Historical Mystery*

# Twin Bluebonnet Ranch Mysteries

*1 Hour Mysteries*

Teachers, Tricks, and Time Capsules

Silent Nights and Shoplifting

Antiques, Alibis, and Auctions

Rodeo, Ransom and Fireworks

Ghostwriters and Gravediggers

Secrets, Lies, and Poisonberry Pies

Friday Night Frights

Turkey, Thievery, and Twins

Sleuths, Sabotage, and Sandcastles

# Heist Society Investigates

*A Roaring Twenties Mystery*

<u>Death by Flapper</u> (Book 1)

<u>Death by Fortune</u> (Book 2)

<u>Death by Matchmaker</u> (Book 3)

<u>Death by Midnight</u> (Book 4)

<u>Death by Railway</u> (Book 5)

<u>Death by Mistletoe</u> (Book 6)

# Robinson Family Detective Agency

*A Humorous Cozy Mystery*

<u>Red Herrings & Pink Flamingos</u>

<u>McGuffins & Birdies</u>

A Hoax & a Hex

A Patsy & a Pastry

A Trick & a Pony

A Masterpiece & a Murder

## Anthologies

A Flock of an Alibi, A Campsite of Culprits,

A Vacation of Mischief, A Festival of Forensics,

A Bookworm of a Suspect, A Haunting of Revenge,

A Beach of a Crime, Once Upon a Halloween

Milton Keynes UK
Ingram Content Group UK Ltd.
UKHW011036201123
432908UK00005BA/712

9 798223 627029